Listen With Your Eyes

*"Reading gives us someplace to go
when we have to stay where we are."*
~ Mason Cooley

C Wayne Pasemko

*I think new writers are too worried
it has been said all before. Sure it has, but not by you.*
– Asha Dornfest

Special thanks to my patient editor, my spouse, Ellen Carlisle

Vorona Verse

Verseology

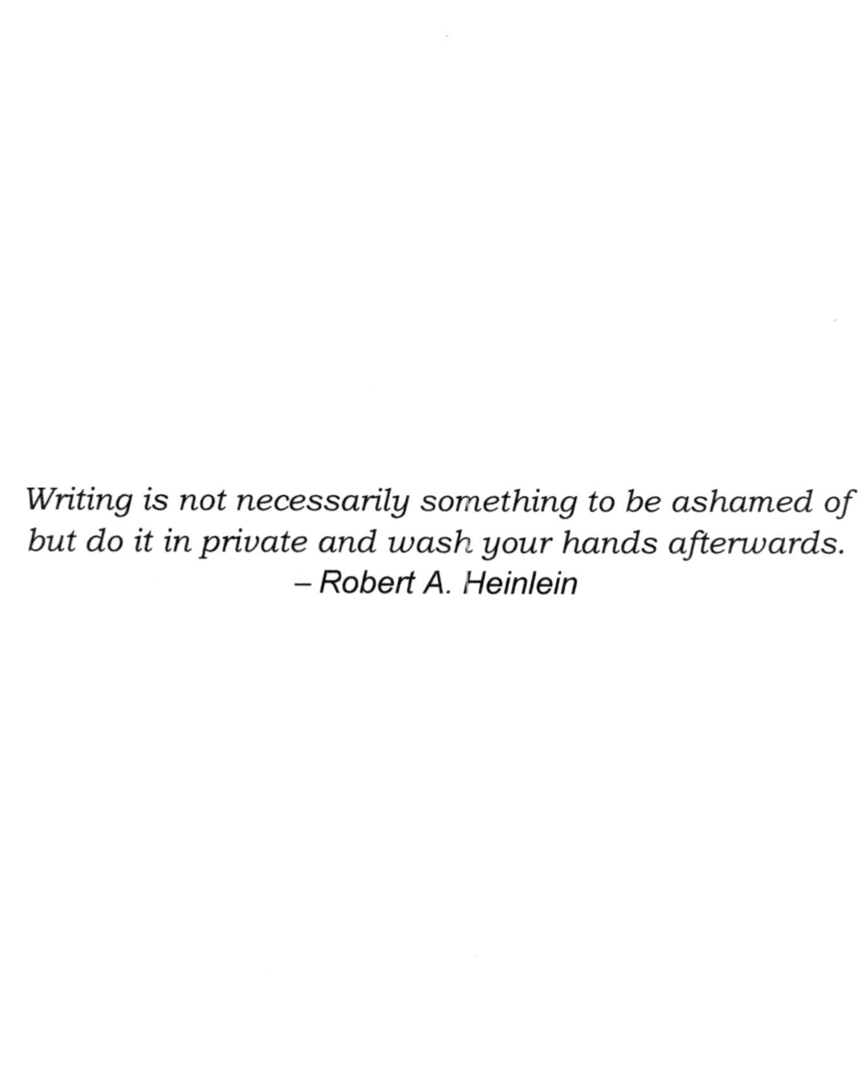

*Writing is not necessarily something to be ashamed of
but do it in private and wash your hands afterwards.*
– Robert A. Heinlein

Prairie Life

*"I was born on the prairies where the wind blew free
and there was nothing to break the light of the sun.
I was born where there were no enclosures."*
- Geronimo

*"Everything in you is open, desolate and level; your squat
towns barely protrude in the midst of the plains...there is
nothing to tempt or enchant the onlooker's gaze. But what is
this inscrutable, mysterious force that draws me to you? "*
- Nikolai Gogol

Redcoat Trail

1884, Fort Dufferin, 300-man
horse mounted constabulary
Parades westward, destination
distant Fort Whoop Up

Resplendent in vermillion coats
white helmets and gauntlets,
black boots, gray breeches
Enfield carbines, an impressive sight

George French, senior officer,
proud of 'spit and polish' command
Contingent made of 6 divisions,
each with distinctive horses;
"A" Division dark bay,
"B" dark browns, "C" chestnuts
"D" grays, "E" blacks, "F" light bays,

North West Mounted Police
Ride into Canadian history
A thin red line across
vast prairie landscape
A mile long support column

Orders: stop whiskey trade,
befriend Indian tribes,
establish law in the west
800-mile journey over desolate
badlands, grasslands, river valleys
spring-fed lakes, pine forests

Suffer scarcity of water and food,
heat, dust, biting insects, dysentery,
death of horses and cattle, getting lost
A moving hardship, men in distress

Arrive Roche Percée, 240 miles
Several days of needed rest,
A Division' sent north west
to Fort Edmonton

B, C, D Divisions push on
junction of Bow and Belly
780 miles, unable to proceed
Enlist help of Metis scout, Jerry Pots
guides column to Fort Whoop-Up

NWMP draw near, whisky traders take flight,
with western tribes smoke peace pipe
Mission accomplished, no fighting, no death
NWMP establish Canadian law in the west

Based on _Red Coat Trail_ at turtleandtoad.com

Saturday Night Fever
(Circa 1955)

Nightfall, Saturday night
a rural prairie town
Under autumn fading light
they come from all around

Farm folk in cars and pickups
to the community hall
Children and grownups
anticipate first movie of the fall

Before black and white tv
when radio reigned supreme
Once a month played a movie
Vivid technicolor dream

Treats and movie for a quarter
Leave the mundane for 15 cents
A fantasy world transformer
Folks held in delightful suspense

Delivered by a Greyhound
Dreamtime in spinning reels
Leaving us children spellbound
Tonight we're head over heels

Outdoor Rink
(Circa 1957)

A clear evening in January
Walk the frigid white prairie
A youngster afoot in his town
For the outdoor rink I'm bound

Grainy snow squeaks underfoot
Carry an apple, some edible loot
Steamy mist from my mouth
Starry sky a glow in the south

Across Whitaker's icy yard
Past Murray's shack, life lived hard
By Anglican church I top the hill
Below a sight that elicits a thrill

A glistening jewel, town centre piece
To me a light flooded masterpiece
An oasis bright in a desert of dark
The rink ice a whiteness so stark

Transformed by a galvanic sprite
Six light poles, turn night into light
My ears delight, skating music
An inward smile, so therapeutic

Change shack heating with scented smoke
On the skates, push off with power stroke
With joy and vigor my skates find the stride
On ice I ride, with youthful abandon glide

Hometown

I pine for prairie town of formative years
Return to the past my soul haplessly yearns
Six decades a small-town boy haunted
For the past fixate, memories undaunted

Unremarkable middling farm settlement
The young yearned for their betterment
From its environs to the city to roam
Older folks remained, 'home sweet home'

On our town we turned our backs
First, they came for the railway station,
grain elevators and finally the tracks
Some said, "Modernity that's what town lacks"

'Growth' trite cliché, town council homily
Enlarge, enrich, diversify the community
The Edmonton Garrison, an opportunity
Populate the town with soldier's family

Gone forever the quaint village of the fifties
along with memories of interest only to me
Recollections delicious, some bitter gritty
Live in the past under shade of leafless tree

But I can see the sun's settin' fast
And just like they say, nothing good ever lasts..
Go on now and say goodbye to my town, to my town
I can see the sun has gone down on my town,
on my town, Goodnight

Iris Dement, My Town

Tractors

Pioneers and sturdy workhorses
turned prairie land into fields of grain
Farmers and mechanical workhorses
grew grainy wealth, food to sustain

Tractors the lynchpin, the mainstay
A simple, single purposed contraption
To rural life opened a gateway
For the farmer a benefaction

Tractors of the forties to sixties
Attest, 'form follows function'
Shorn of comforts, accessories
Simple design limits malfunction

Known by a host of monikers;
Cockshut, Allis Chalmers
International Harvester
Massey, Case, John Deere
The lesser known Oliver

Single, vital service to proffer
Pull, drag, yank cultivators,
harrows, disks, seeders
harvesters, plows and swathers
Ensuring a farm family prosper

Working life an endless circle
Tractor, farmer merry-go-round
Blue print for farming universal
Encircle, cultivate verdant ground
A bond, until both lay horizontal

Mother Goose

I see you, proud mother with your brood
Searching the grass for breakfast food
Parading behind our back yard fence
On display your caring maternal sense

Six tiny dune-coloured goslings
no longer 'stay-at-home' nestlings
Their safe home they are leaving
to follow you bobbing and weaving

Like tiny ships in a grassy sea
Mother goose head of Admiralty
Their masts, tiny darting heads
Paddling on feet with webs
In time mom captains her flock to their nest
The maiden voyage a family success

The Gander

I see you proud father of adolescent brood
Your gander led parade; a warmup, a prelude
to the right of passage, the coming of age
With newly formed wings, the adult stage

Dad takes to the air shows how to fly
Flapping and fluttering they give it a try
Flights, 20 feet long with a 10-foot ceiling
some aborted take offs, a crash landing

No time to squawk better take stock
Must earn a place in a V shaped flock
After many tires they earn their wings
Freed of Mother Goose's apron strings

Fearlessly flying high above the neighborhood
In formation a winged honking brotherhood
Soon will depart on your southern quest
Thank you Honkers for being our guest

'"Geese always support each other. When a goose gets injured two birds always accompany it down to the ground. Just as geese do, we must support each other."
- Emma Hayes

Monday Blues

Clothes pins in hand, wet clothes in the other
Reaching for the clothesline feeling a shiver
Blue Monday, wintertime on the prairie
Frigid cold housewives ought not tarry

Clothes carefully pinned by reddened hands
Wind whipped icy snow cutting like desert sands
Three more loads to wash, rinse and hangout
Her work unsung, no acclaim or family 'shout out'

As first mate anchors the household ship
Her family blind to her Monday hardship
Bone chilling work carried out with regularity
Loved ones hung out to dry in frozen effigy

Prairie Wind

On the plains an enduring feature
Resides a moody restless creature
Origins ancient, countless millennium
Epochs predating the Plains Indian

Unannounced from north and west
Prairie's relentless uninvited guest
The ceaseless wind, a mixed blessing
Gentle breezes and gustily pressing

Summer wind sends in retreat
mosquito clouds, stifling heat
Creating rippling oceans of grain
A squall ushers thunderous rain

Northern winds drive snow and sleet
Howling to a freezing fearful beat
Snow swept into shapes that grow,
undulating white desert of snow

Prairie wind, beast and friend
With it's breath we must contend
Restless companion gentle or scary
Our love-hate bond on the prairie

Storytelling

"Humans think in stories, and we try to make sense of the world by telling stories."
- Yuval Noah Harari

"Some stories are true that never happened."
- Elie Wiesel

Fire Flowers

The Gathering
Late evening, they come in uncounted number
Eager for a night of wonder and thunder
Blissfully ignorant of the drama to ensue
Known to Greek scholars and only a few

Story line familiar and timeless
Reoccurring theme that is countless
Unrequited love the plot centrepiece
The opening scene is ancient Greece

Ancient Greece
Chloris known as the Greek nymph of flowers
An intimate of Artemis, a deity with vast powers
Among Artemis's many roles is Goddess of chastity
Persona, she assumes fervently and tirelessly

Enter Anteros with a passion for Chloris
His loving entreaties she is helpless
To her friend Artemis does confide
she yearns to be Anteros's loving bride

Although it will break her friend's heart
Artemis schemes to tear the lovers apart
Diabolical schemes are soon unfurled
Into the darkness Anteros is hurled

The love birds forever torn asunder
Matters of the heart do not surrender
Anteros's love for Chloris will not die
He seeks his maiden in the night sky

Fire Flowers
Here to marvel at the night sky artworks
The much-anticipated July 1st fireworks
A night of pyrotechnic coloured rain
Some enthusiasts know them by name

The dazzling golden Brocade Crown
opens the pyrotechnic countdown
The Crackle, Strobe and Fish the next acts
Favourites of pyromaniacs

Hidden in the darkness grieving Atheros
High in the night sky the forlorn Chloris
Like a tracer bullet an arrow pierces the night
Atheros message of love takes flight

Chloris responds with the showy Peony
It's bright red burst for all folks to see
Two pink Chrysanthemums blanket the sky
So beautiful, lovesick Anteros begins to cry

The show is over the folks tiredly disperse
Never to know of the lover's endless curse
And so it goes, once yearly for thousands of years
Unrequited love played to music of the spheres

    *Fire flowers – Japanese name for fireworks
    **Anteros – God of unrequited love

*"We are like fireworks... Rising, shining, and finally scattering
and fading. So until that moment comes when we vanish
like fireworks... Lets us sparkle brightly, Always."*
~ Tite Kubo

Hidden Army

The Year of the Tiger, 1974
A found relic opens an ancient door
A farmer digging a well for water
Unearthed underground squatter

Two thousand years in lightless solitude
Standing in stoic servitude
At his feet to bow and genuflect
Emperor Quin to serve and protect

Rooted in place, comrade and kin
Each a humanoid mannequin
Living a netherworld existence
Maintain their ranks with persistence

Eight thousand, the emperor's army
A lifeless life stark and eerie
Warriors, soundless guardians
Duty bound afterlife barbarians

With horses and fine armament
Stand in battle ready deployment
The emperor's quest for immortality
Seals the army's fate with finality

In perpetuity they face the east
Never to savor love or feast
Evermore the sun will rise
On an army that never dies

Mechanical Man

I am an authentic mechanical man
Predate android, cyborg, the moon rover
Fabricated by hand from a 1970s plan
Three times I have been tweaked, made over

Like God, man made me in his own image
I'm bespoke, one of a kind, first in my lineage
Skeletal frame of rebar, springs for muscles
Battery power lights my lights, makes me hustle

Strung with two miles of wiring from Canadian Tire
30 meters duct tape, parts from a clothes dryer,
solenoids, transistors, resistors, doodads and a gizmo
Brain programmed to be smug, somewhat machismo

No digital codes, hard drives, implanted computers or floppy
I am old school, tough durable stout and happy
My skin half inch stainless steel, little heavy at 333
I clatter squeak and clank, move along at two miles an hour
Back to the shop, mount second battery double my power

Suffer power surge, left arm flays about denting my head
Dubbed a useless heap of junk my metallic life is dead
My dismal performance makes creators moan and shutter
"No commercial value, won't pay for our bread and butter"

Hauled to a farm, an out building, dust, bird poop smothered
Hoping it won't be seasons and decades before rediscovered
Did they forget the whole is greater than the sum of its parts?
Almost a humanoid, they coldly broke my two plastic hearts

Living Waters

Solitary figure adrift on a boat
Constant struggle to keep it afloat
Tirelessly and doggedly he rows his dory
Life on the water the plot of this story

Decades spent charting these waters
Unceasing rowing is all that matters
Heading dictated by the outgoing tide
Pulled ever closer to the far side

Often enveloped by the murk of a fog
With oars in hand continues to slog
Out of the gloom boats come into sight
Each piloted by one, a mariner's plight

Solitary figures manning each craft
Propelled by the incessant tide's draft
Few set course to the distant shore
Most meander, journey's end they abhor

Sometimes becalmed, seemingly without motion
"As idle as a painted ship, upon a painted ocean" *
When the water is calm and glassy smooth
He harkens back to the time of his youth

He ponders the loss of the love of his life
She sickened, faded, died under the knife
To replace his First Mate, he took on another
A Second Mate to love and help him recover

When a Nor' wester threatened their boat
She jumped ship, 'goodbye' a handwritten note
Deep in reflection on his time on the water
He wonders why he rejected his daughter

Continues the journey in troubling thought
Pondering the mysteries the water brought
Unscripted, relentlessly moves the skiff
He will tenaciously row until cold and stiff

Journey's end is in fog shrouded sight
Deathly quiet and devoid of life-giving light
The time is nigh to draw his last breath
Few he will leave saddened, bereft

The odyssey is over, the final ride
This sailor crossed over to the other side

*Samuel Taylor Coldwell
- Rhyme of the Ancient Mariner

Mars Vacation

Taking a trip to the Red Planet
with my good friend Janet
Plan blast off Christmas eve
A 3-month holiday reprieve

Pin-stripe ten-meter sky rocket
Plugged into kitchen electric socket
We're so excited about our trip
Have started packing up the ship

Janet is sewing new pajamas
crafted from the hide of llamas
She's knitted matching sweaters
Our initials in big block letters

Packing sandwiches and coffee
Three pounds of creamy toffee
We have furry, lace-up boots
to match pastel Michelin suits

Frolic on red sandy beaches
Hope to avoid Martian leaches
No travel insurance beyond moon
That's OK, cosmos virus immune

I have a hidden reason for this trip
Can't confide in Janet, she will flip
No need to say words rude or brusk
Shrink the ego of 'know it all' Musk

To take him down as I plan it
Beat Elon Musk to the red planet

Off Centre

*"I can't understand
why people are frightened of new ideas.
I'm frightened of the old ones."*
- John Cage

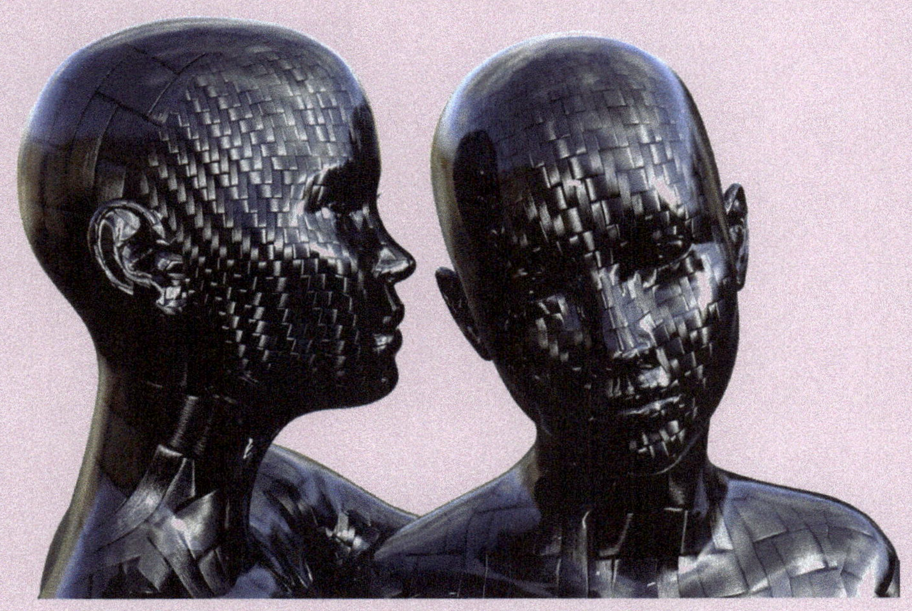

*"Expose your ideas to the danger of controversy.
Speak your mind and fear less the label
of 'crackpot' than the stigma of conformity."*
– Thomas J. Watson

*"The art of writing is the art of discovering
what you believe."*
– Gustave Flaubert

Disbelief

What if…
Our worldview is out of focus
One's foundational beliefs are wrong
We're standing on intellectual quicksand
Our belief system is bogus, counterfeit
History as we know it is riddled with untruths
Historians, scientists befuddled by the unexplained

What if…
Death is not the end of consciousness
Things do go bump in the night
The USA is not the world's beacon of hope
Free unlimited energy is being hidden from mankind
Semi-human beings live undetected in the wilderness
The explanation of the 9/11 collapse of the twin towers is farcical.
The ancients had technologies superior to modern man
We are not alone in the universe
There is little factual evidence that Jesus existed
NATO expansion is a contributing factor to war in Ukraine
Climate change is a humankind extinction time bomb
Alien lifeforms have been and/or are now amongst us.
We are not the person we like to think we are

What if…

The US stops its global military interventions
Bill Gates, Elon Musk, Oprah Winfrey, get far less 'air time'
Russians overthrow their empire obsessed, homicidal leader
Canadian aboriginals stop the clamor for land and funding
Canadian governments stop giving in to their demands
The RCMP get better training
Religious organisations pay their fair share of taxes
Conservatives stop aping the American right
Progressives are more judicious in their use of cancel culture
NHL players made less money than a brain surgeon
Stop sanctions as a means of war on peaceful countries
People in leadership positions drop 'I' from their vocabulary
Elon Musk rockets off to Mars and never comes back

What if..
I stop whining and shut the f..k up

Anglophone

In my brain dwells an anglophone
In a single language on I drone
Thoughts limited, a singularity
Think same thoughts with regularity

Hidden thoughts I cannot think
Pools of knowledge do not drink
Ideas beyond my imagination
Emotions felt but lack expression
Intellect constrained as a unilingual
Lack thoughts, voices of the multilingual

Cybernetics

We are on a journey fellow traveller
Lock step within our demographic
Assigned by a digital calculator
A digit, a mathematical statistic

No longer a being with human agency
A test subject of predictive analytic
Manipulated, exploited with blatancy
by marketers vile and parasitic

With their precise panoptic metric
corporatists employ the digital whore
The learned and competent selected
catalyze maximize profits to soar

Awaken, rise feisty digital Luddite
Autonomous thinking man is waning
Be prepared, fight the good fight
Reject cyber solutions life constraining

Oppose digital methods of technocrats
that mock humanism and democracy
Let them face this sobering fact
we are more than a digital commodity

Climbers

From afar they look like insects
Single-file up a leaden rock
Barely perceptible living objects
Frequently slowed to deadlock

Alpinist and Mountaineer
Rock jocks mastering fear
Extreme sport evangelists
Death defying enthusiasts

The chosen few who don't fail
Summit Everest the holy grail
Join mountaineering elite
Most face painful defeat

Mountain guides take their dime
Forty-thousand to make the climb
Sign up all those willing to pay
The inept rarely turned away
Sherpa do the heavy lifting
Basic pay their lives risking
Carry supplies set up camps
Fix route; ropes, ladders, clamps

Hundreds of would-be alpinists
Green novices, a few the finest
Share the same crazed plan
Face a climbing traffic jam

Extreme winds, frostbite
Hypothermia, loss of sight
Altitude sickness need overcome
or to deadly trauma succumb

Must transverse the death zone
to reach the Everest capstone
With luck the grim reaper defied
310 followed the dream and died

A mountain to climb and tame
Earn ten minutes of fleeting fame
Few care or know their name
Is this quest not quite insane?

"Everest doesn't attract a whole lot of well-balanced folks. The self-selection process tends to weed out the cautious and the sensible in favor of those who are single-minded and incredibly driven. Which is a big reason the mountain is so dangerous."
- Jon Krakauer

Extreme Philanthropy

Bungee jumping, freediving
kitesurfing, ice climbing
cave diving, mountaineering
hang gliding, off-the-track skiing
Playtime for adrenaline junkies
Impress yourself and your buddies

In the groove, death defying antics
The 'juice' of extreme sports fanatics
Dare devil stunts leave us in awe
Thrilling performance without a flaw

The 'shelf life' is for the young
Reach mid-thirties then you're done
Bravery and skill there is no doubt
But is this what life's all about?

Perhaps you ought to audition
for another form of competition
Harness your competitive drive
to help humanity sustain and thrive

Create a philanthropic plan
to support your fellow man
Establish a social connector
join hands with the third sector

A solo or team competition
of a like-minded coalition
Extreme philanthropy games
contests by various names*

Spirited rivalry for the common good
Competing in selfless brotherhood

*Ocean/Island cleanup project
Establish desert green belt
Refugee camp tent erection
Natural disaster cleanup
Reforestation of burnt-out areas, Etc.

"Philanthropy is commendable, but it must not cause the philanthropist to overlook the circumstances of economic injustice which make philanthropy necessary."
~ Martin Luther King, Jr.

The Truth is Out There

They reside above us; flashing, streaking, looping
Some hold stationary orbits, on course never deviating
Scientists, Hackers, Gamers search them with browsers
NASA has thousands of images, solar system of treasures

Their presence observed since recorded history
In near space enthrall mankind with mystery
They live above us perhaps among us
Decades of debate, speculation, much to discuss

Aliens, galactic explorers, inter-stellar interlopers
Black hole navigators, time warpers, time travelers
A myriad of reputable sightings, people of sound mind;
astronauts, pilots, cops, doctors, cosmonauts, reporters
speak of encounters of the first, second and third kind

All manner of craft; balls of light, irregular shapes, saucers
triangles, multi-story ships, hovering cigars, Foo fighters
May possess intelligence, behavior, bodies beyond imaging
Perhaps features, smells, voices that are maddening

Where, how and why they come citizens don't know
The ruling elite hiding info, dark state secrets in tow?
In time the truth to disclose, aliens to expose

Our World

*"Either men will learn to live like brothers,
or they will die like beasts."
- Max Lerner*

*"The whole problem with the world is
that fools and fanatics are always so certain of
themselves, and wiser people so full of doubts."
- Bertrand Russell*

Stealth Killers

It's quiet, peaceful in the village
Folks go about their daily tasks
Saadat hangs out the family laundry
Vahedi is baking unleavened bread

Faizal toils in the fields
Yousef is teaching an Arabic class
Ambeer and Amaan converse over morning tea
Young children play in dusty streets
Call to prayer, faithful bow on prayer mats

An ear-splitting blast, superheated shockwave
The ground shakes, children scream
People in the street hurled to the ground,
Buildings explode ejecting metal fragments,
brick shrapnel and body parts, fires erupt
A lethal drone strike, invisible and invincible
More innocents for the collateral damage ledger

Horrific burns, shattered limbs, pierced ear drums
Disfigurements, some crippled for life
The loss of loved ones, ever present anxiety and fear
Homes to rebuild, shattered lives to mend

Afghanistan, Pakistan, Syria, Iraq, Somalia, Yemen
Targets of relentless lethal drone attacks
'Extrajudicial killings,' legalese for death and mayhem,
The 'imminent threat' hoax cover for drone murderers

The west's grim reaper exacts it's pound of flesh
Slayers at computer screens, advanced tech to wage war
An automated killing field; cruel, inhuman and illegal

Picasso I

Closing of the 19th century
You stand paintbrush in hand
A detailed, pictorial treasury
painted on canvas in longhand

Artfully, detail life as you knew it
Colours warm, in accordant harmony
Care, humanity, painted as befit
Life portrayed, carefully and honestly

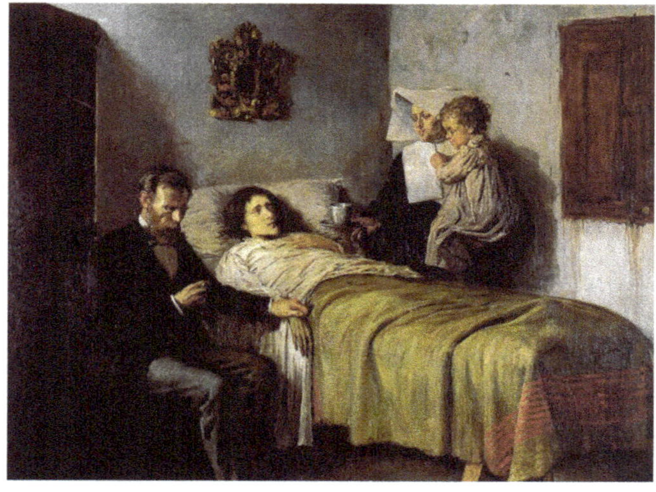

Picasso II

The 20th century, discordance and chaos
Great War, men mired in mud and blood
A world of mayhem, civility a loss
A river of wretched tears, a flash flood

Post war paintings, sigh of the times
A woman suffering, distorted, weeping
Canvases, perplexing figures and lines
Vivid figures from canvas
leaping

Faces, bodies twisted, contorted
Portent of our lives, the future?
From our humanity aborted
In short supply, love and nurture

Man alienated from self and others
Picasso paintings, a cautionary tale
Fissures between, sisters and brothers
Need heed painted voice, risk humane fail

Middle East Racism *

"Racism is man's gravest threat to man
maximum of hatred for a minimum of reason"**
Most persistent human vice to ban
Hatred of the other is always in season

Group hatred for 'the other' world wide
Antisemitism, Islamophobia flourish
Ethnocentrism, xenophobia haven't died
Will hate for the other ever perish?

The Saudis hate Syrians
Japanese despise Okinawans
Neo-Nazis loathe people of colour
The West detests Russians
Tutsis abhor the Hutus
White folk resent aboriginals

The Zionist reasons with his fellow occupiers,
"God's chosen are of course superior"
Proclaiming; "Palestinians are inferior,
too dishonest, stupid, lazy to be achievers"

Like enemy in a war, the other is objectified
stripped of humanity, rights, dignity
Hate, humiliate, kill, to humanity desensitized
Talk of democracy, peace a farcical parody

"I will fight the down trodden to keep my way of life,
Indifferent to who's back I break or hyde,
Will suppress with bombs and bloody knife
I am justified, God is on my side."

Written before the Palestine—Israel War
*** First two lines, a quote by Abraham Joshua Herchel,*
American Polish Rabbi

Poor Kids

Poverty, 360 degrees of misery
Visited on God's precious children
Kids bereft of life necessities
Income gap, greed the villain

Poverty, a life ravaging hell hound
A life of despair to scarcity bound
Poor kids, lives harshly impacted
Their plight largely hidden, redacted

Impoverishment, a childhood stressed
with early development growth messed
Prefrontal cortex, hippocampus damaged
Toxic stress, brain delayed and savaged

Health, education outcomes, second rate
Poverty and crime, a statistical correlate
Poor children, a life of want, envy and despair
Try not turn away, feel the pain if you dare

Give them a hand, a heaven sent prayer
Pray our children don't go there.

Viral Hubris

Sans wars, pestilence, starvation
Few cataclysmic events accrue
"…just talkin' bout my generation" *
Few national disasters to rue

Coronavirus, a chastening
Blessed generation, looming Waterloo
For some a divine reckoning
Lives in turmoil, living askew

Baby Boomer comeuppance
belies our unprepared stupidity
Life's frailty denied, willful ignorance
Will we learn from our culpability?

** The Who, My Generation*

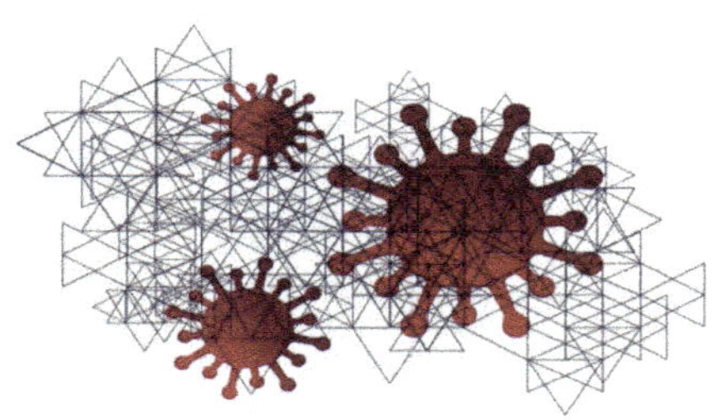

*Isn't it Odd…9/11 **

Isn't it odd that there was not a single scientist on the 9/11 Commission and the editor of Fire Engineering magazine called their investigation "…a half-baked farce…"?

Isn't it odd that not a single steel frame skyscraper has collapsed into its footprint before or after 9/11 apart from those brought down by controlled demolition?

Isn't it odd that Bldg. Seven, a 47-floor steel framed building collapsed into its footprint supposedly from an office fire?

Isn't it odd that the twin towers were designed to withstand plane collisions like the ones that purportedly brought the towers down?

Isn't it odd that molten steel, associated with controlled demolitions, was found in the debris of the collapsed towers and was never mentioned in the 9/11 Commission Report (CR)?

Isn't it odd that perimeter steel columns weighing several tons were ejected horizontally 500 to 600 feet, when the towers collapsed?

Isn't it odd that the 9/11 CR claimed there was no evidence that explosions (associated with a demolition) occurred just before the towers came down when over 100 NY firefighters along with journalists, police and citizens reported hearing explosions?

Isn't it odd that the collapse of the Twin Towers and Bldg. 7 have all the hallmarks of a controlled demolition – sudden onset, straight down, rapid constant acceleration, total collapse, pulverization, and dust clouds?

Isn't it odd that not one of the four 'hijacked' plane's pilots or copilots 'squawked' the universal hijack code, which they are trained to do and takes 2 to 3 seconds to send?

Isn't odd that the wreckage of the plane that crashed near Shanksville, Pennsylvania was found scattered up to eight miles from the site of impact?

Isn't it odd that the 9/11 commission, FBI and the Whitehouse did not provide any hard evidence that Osama Bin laden was the mastermind of 9/11?

Isn't it odd that the hijacker, Hani Hanjour credited with flying an airliner into the pentagon, which required a highly skilled 270-degree pivot maneuver, was known by his flight school to be an incompetent pilot? One employee stated that "he could not fly at all".

Isn't it odd that over 3600 architects and engineers, and hundreds of pilots, have signed petitions calling for a new and thorough investigation of the events of 9/11?

Isn't it odd that that what is stated here is only a fraction of the bizarre and odd events of 9/11?

*Isn't it Odd…9/11 is based on research of the following sources:
 9/11 Unmasked, David Ray Griffin & Elizabeth Woodworth,
Olive Branch Press
https://www.ae911truth.org
https://pilotsfor911truth.org*

> *"True patriotism hates injustice in its own land*
> *more than anywhere else."*
> *— Clarence Darrow*

Spoil Sport

Ice hockey our national pastime, a Canadian passion
Only in the summer heat does it go out of fashion
Old school hockey played on sloughs, lakes, rinks and rivers
Often skating with cold feet, nose, ears and shivers

An exuberant winter sport practiced in its purest form
before money and greedy interests became the norm
The game transformed and sold as a commodity
Morphed into just another commercial novelty
Predatory financiers saw it as way to get rich
and turned our passion into a money-making pitch

Overhyped players as part of the mix
get bloated contracts as part of the fix
Seeking fame and even greater pay
Wayne packs up for the Kings of LA
Deserting a welcoming supportive city
spurns his loyal fans, such a pity

Bettman, NHL hired gun and big fish
does the owners bidding as they wish
The slick bagman and puppet master
ensures greenbacks roll in ever faster
While the NHL pulls in over two billion
poor old Gary earns a paltry seven million

Told we must have a pro franchise
or city face second class demise
Public funds to help build a splashy venue
Subsidies for the rich is hardly new

Overpriced tickets, concessions and merch
leave 'Joe Six-Pack' in the lurch
Pristine rink boards once painted white
now a brand pimping marketing sight
Season tickets domain of business elite
Tax write-offs rewarded with a box seat

A sport that repeatedly stops the play
to allow advertisers to have their say
For faithful fans of hockey
an appalling form of mockery

Our game turned into a commercialized spectacle
For many hockey lovers it's reprehensible

*"...when I was a kid, my dad would not let us on the ice
without hockey sticks, because of this insane fear
we would become figure skaters!"*
- Norm MacDonald

"It's more fun to be playing hockey than doing anything else."
- Connor McDavid

The Stork and the Bear *

The White Stork nests on the plains
Fields bountiful with sunflowers, grains
Home for hundreds of generations
Borders, statehood respected by nations

To the east a land lusting vengeful bear
Connives and plots the Stork to snare
Under the whip of crazed bear wrangler
'Stalin lite' war addicted bird strangler

Threatening with its oft used battle axe
Armed with artillery the bear attacks
Stork pleads help countries west
Bird begs send weapons your very best

Ciconia no match for mad carnivore
Stork prepares for a bloody war
Needed missiles, tanks and lady luck
or bear will ravage and feathers pluck

Messages Hedgehog, the NATO alliance
Please help with struggle of defiance
Risk being beaten, throttled by the neck
Bruin savaging nest, a shattered wreck

Hedgehog takes bravado vocal stance
With growling bear refuses to dance
Postures with soldiers on eastern flank
Sends no troops, not a 'war loving' Yank

Joining Hedgehog, Swan and Blackbird
Stork shut out, 'scram' the final word
Hedgehog fears mauling by riled bear
Hubris talk, safe distance from his lair

Will cut off investments for the bear
No goods and services go there
Hedgehog cheers encouragement
Stands by bird's dismemberment

Stork tragically loosing war of attrition
Bear seizes land won by aggression
Blood-soaked empire the prize of war
Stork sacrificed, no longer to soar

*White Stork - national bird of Ukraine
Ciconia - scientific name for Stork
Whooping Swan - national bird of Finland
Eurasian Blackbird - national bird of Sweden
Bear - national animal of Russia
Hedgehog - Eisenhower's nickname for NATO*

Czar Vladimir the War Criminal
aka Stalin Lite

Their Children, Our Children

Something is not Right

THEIR children live in tents,
shacks, huts, hovels, under trees
In cold, wet conditions
under a 40-degree sun
Camps often unsafe, dirty
Few make-shift schools, no parks

OUR children have warm, soft beds
comforters, their own rooms, decorated
walls, living area

THEIR children sleep on dirt floors
perhaps on a carpet, warmth from
thin blankets, close bodies of their siblings
Children live with family in one room or tent
unsafe, overused dirty outdoor bathrooms
water carried home in pails

OUR children have closets
crammed with sweaters
blouses, jeans, dress clothes
skirts, dresses, shirts
t-shirts, jackets, coats,

THEIR children have one pair
hand-me-down broken shoes
Raggedy worn pants, ill-fitting sweaters,
Stained, torn light jackets,
ripped underwear
Girls wear passed down sweaters,
traditional tattered skirts, broken
down runners, perhaps a bracelet

OUR children have stuffed animals,
action figures, dolls, Lego sets
ear buds, smart phones, bicycles
electronic toys, tablets, laptops
Xboxes, sporting gear & uniforms
kittens, goldfish, dogs

THEIR children have almost nothing;
a rag doll, coloured pencil,
battered soccer ball,
braided string, old jewelry
a stick for whittling, a ripped
school book, a small keep-sake

OUR children play soccer,
hockey, have music lessons, tutors,
go to birthday parties, sleep overs
attend church, school functions
hang at the mall, go shopping, movies

THEIR children have few
organized activities, play with
siblings and neighbour children, few have
spending money, adults share
small amount nuts, dates, pistachios

OUR children eat hamburgers
down pop, stuff fries. slurp spaghetti,
wolf ice cream treats, chicken fingers
pizza, pastries, mom prepared meals
Some kids even eat fresh fruit
and vegetables, drink milk

THEIR children often go to bed hungry
Mother prepares rations of starchy foods –
beans, rice, flour for flat bread
some cooking oil, few onions, potatoes
Few fresh vegetables, fruit or meat that
require refrigeration, powdered milk,
limited quantities of dates to treat kids
Mom and dad enjoy tea once a day,
sometimes with sugar, never with fresh milk

OUR children are loved
by parents and grandparents
Many children have mom and dad, one home
Others 'ping pong' between mom and dad
Some children live in blended families
Many children raised by a single parent

THEIR children have loving parents
uncles, aunts, grandparents if they
haven't been blown to bits,
crushed, burned to death or lost
Extended family that loves them
Those who are left do their best
to care & nurture

OUR children have prospects
a future of stability, abundance,
education and health care

THEIR children have little hope
growing without schools, health care
community role models, men with work
stability, a sense of safety,
Homes turned to rubble, infrastructure
decimated, lack funds to rebuild

THEIR children have something that
ours don't - severe anxiety, depression
war induced PTSD,

Children ask, what is our future?
Worried parents have no answer

Something is not Right

Human Condition

*"We see the world through the
lens of all our experiences;
that is a fundamental part
of the human condition."
- Madeleine M. Kunin*

Life's Book

Who are you? What are you?
A galling and baffling question
An inquiry many of us eschew
'Identity' for some an obsession

Mufti-layered fabrics form the 'self'
An interwoven mix of psychic threads
A hand-made costume in which to dwell
Grow to maturity, earn social creds

Maintain editorial control life's book
Review for mistakes, correct as needed
Your life a work in progress, a sketch book
A living memoir, 'warts and all' unimpeded

Your persona writ large, a personal novel
Gain rightful place on life's bookshelf
A well bound script won't unravel
The subtext; 'know yourself"
and "To thy own self be true" *

** Polonius, in Shakespeare's Hamlet.*

Hypocrite

I live the life of a hypocrite
In the light of day an atheist
During the dark prone to waiver

In daily life, health and well being
my stance on the deity is resolute
No God, omnipotent loving all seeing
Life of Christ theologically in dispute
Christianity tenuous way of believing
pagan rituals, myths that took root

Under the light of day, an apostate, an atheist
In the shadows, dark places of life I waiver
Transforming into a God fearing theist
Agnostic declarations fall out of favour

I pray for redemption, compassion, relief,
'And trouble deaf heaven with bootless cries' *
In anguish, a hypocrite a change in belief
Daytime assertions or my dark pleadings,
which are the lies?

* *William Shakespeare- Sonnet 29*

*"I would rather live my life as if there is a God
and die to find out there isn't, than live as
if there isn't and to die to find out that there is."
- Albert Camus*

Water Memory

Our planet, you and I seventy percent water
Come share a glass of life giving liquid
Let's explore our aquatic marine heritage
Drink deeply from a watershed aquifer

Water, the source of memories, nostalgia
shared recollections, expanded consciousness
Our universal liquid heritage, watery shared humanity
You and I bound with water, l'eau, voda, agua, vatten

Could drinking from divergent sources
account for disagreement, discord, disharmony?
Is it possible cultures are water based,
water holding distinctive memories for each?
Come let us clink our drinking vessels
and drink our fill from the same oasis

Professor Chaplin and Dr Peter Fisher,
editor-in-chief of the journal (Homeopathy)...
Agree that the memory of water, once considered
a scientific heresy, is a reality.   www.elsevier.com

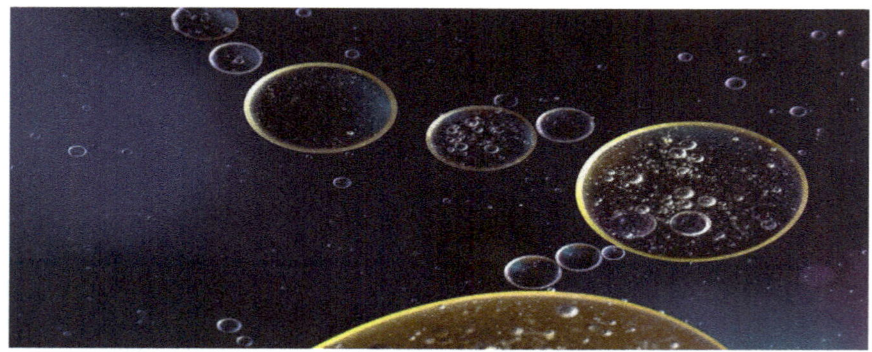

Brave New World

Neurologists, geneticists,
micro and evolution biologists
push the domain of humanists,
artists, poets, romantics

To the former, a mechanistic biosphere
the realm of social engineers
Behavior based on DNA, genetic code,
biochemical states
Nature verses nurture exposed, nature wins

Posit three Bio-systems the basis
of human love and attraction:

Libido charged by chemical stews
of testosterone and estrogen

Attraction is helped along by
adrenaline, dopamine and serotonin

Attachment system reliant on
oxytocin and vasopressin

All this may have a basis in fact,
To which I say, "So what?"
Do we not possess human agency?
Have we not our own peculiarities, yearnings
devoid of what chemical mixture brain present?
Make judgments on beauty,
intelligence, personality, disposition
without biochemical preparation?

Our brave new world, what glories that await
Securing partners based on formulas
Taking the romance out of romance
Turning us into perpetual horny adolescents

Have you forgotten that the human mind
is more than three pounds of gelatinous matter?
The human gestalt is greater than its parts
Have you developed chemical liqueur for the soul?
Thanks, but no thanks, I'll take my living straight

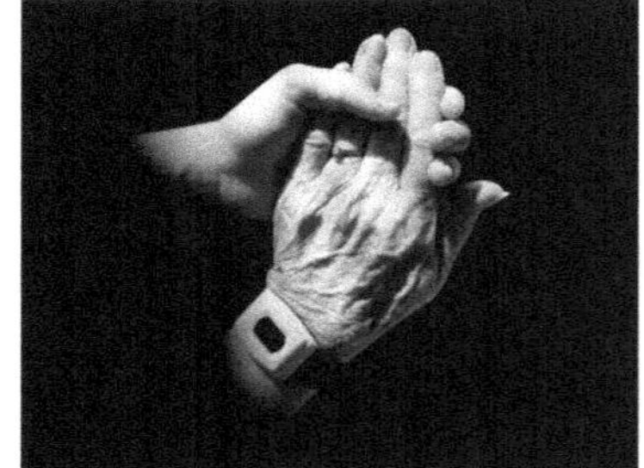

A Mother's Love

To the east she made plans to roam
Province of her birth, a new home
Decades spent away from mother
Place in her heart like no other

With affection home to elderly loved one
Two to reminisce, shared memory rerun
Hope renews mother daughter friendship
Time is short deepen their relationship

Assignments, housework dropped at mom's entreat
Visiting senior's care home often to repeat
Daughter, mother to her failing parent
To motherly love the heir apparent

Two joined in life celebration
A deeply human loving connection

Tonguing

My tongue has its own life
With sharp speech, a verbal flick-knife

On the tip of my tongue
shy words and names get hung

Eloquence my tongue is thrashing
Deserved a good tongue lashing

My tongue firmly in cheek
with words I feint and deke

In verbosity I take much pride
Grovel and stutter when tongue tied

Known as a silver-tongued devil
Manipulating I am top-level

Some folks I annoy, earn their ire
My forked tongue makes me a liar

Gibberish, claptrap, twaddle from my mouth comes
Pure hokum, some call it 'speaking in tongues'

To my better self tongue is merciless
Perhaps would be better off tongueless

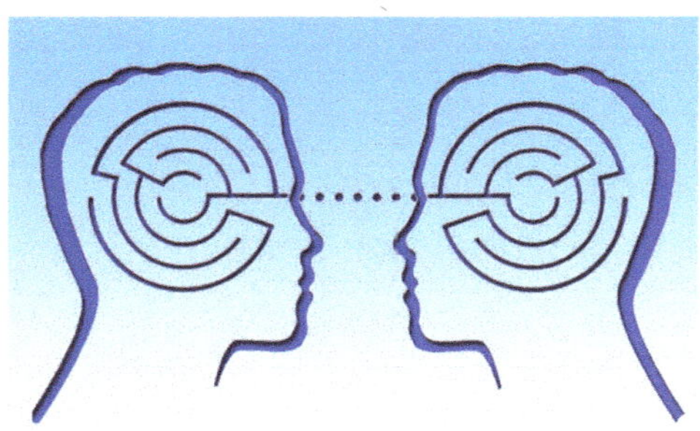

Brainy Us

Where precisely do you live?
Locate the station you broadcast from
Can you position your receiver?
Your location private, fixed, local to you

You and me several inches behind eye sockets
Just above our ears secure within our skull
The centre of our consciousness, your very being
Sensory organs our antennae, outer world feelers

The brain; interpreter, feeler, decider, action taker
Dare to feel the truncated disembodied you
Live In the moment acknowledge you are your head
Feed your head, a gelatin synapses-ridden 3 lb mass

The body in the service of the brain, your existence
Nervous system, organs, tissues, skeleton, muscles
A labyrinth, an interlocking intricate structure
Enable life sustaining, enriching regulating processes

Brain; supreme commander, el commandante, dictator?
Expression of you, your essence you stripped naked?
Beyond mere biology, mind over matter
The mind, greater than the brain, who we really are

In the Moment

Live in the moment, be in the moment
Books written, classes conducted, advice given
Key to living wisely and fully
Free up your soul, live in the 'here and now'

Trendy pop psychology for the 'empty'
Self-proclaimed gurus lucrative wave to ride
Law of Attraction, lifeless exhausted expired
Live in the Moment, pop trend exploitation

Gives rise, "And, how long is a moment?"
A Nano second? - an unintelligible micro thought
Half a second, one, two, three, maybe four?
When does a moment begin, end, the duration?

A moment defines a finite space of time
If not, one moment bleeds into another
A continuum of time, elongated 'here and now'
The moment loses its shape conceptual utility

Fruitless waste of time analyze deep think this notion?
Perhaps there is no gauge, scale for a moment in time
Moments exist on a subjective personal plane
Living in the moment unique to the experience of each

Dream Time

"We gave the Future to the winds,
and slumbered tranquilly in the Present,
weaving the dull world around us into dreams."
- Edgar Allan Poe

Dreamboat

Sure would like to own a boat
Just want to dream as I float
A tiny craft for two and a dog
Flee urbanity, noise and smog

Explore the island, river and lake
Take to the helm like Francis Drake
Track a rootless course, a water snake
Followed by a gentle effervescent wake

Aimlessly follow the dense tree coast line
pausing to heed the lake from time to time
Do her waters have a message for me?
Plot a different course, a new life key?

Pull into a remote cove, commune with nature
Tune in, experience flora's nomenclature
The eraser of night fades the colour of day
Within the hour the black blanket, sun's last ray

The moon rises from the bottom of the lake
It's light reflected in the sky and our wake
Moon and stars aglow in water and sky
I sense, that just perhaps, God is nigh

Altered State

Let me live, thrive in my head
Dream a life before I'm dead
Claim my place in the exotic
Escapades flirting the erotic

Tear the bounds of the real
Entertain thoughts I can feel
Relish the strange, the abnormal
Commune with the paranormal

Oh, for a life of imagination
Sans vexation, frustration
Renew, revitalize life history
imbued with zest and mystery

Trip in a world fantastic
Reality malleable, elastic
Write lyrics for a haunting song
Sung with verve before I'm gone

Compassion

Sins of thoughtless omission
Feeling remorseful contrition
Blind with self to see the other
Deaf to the needs of a brother
Sister teach me compassion
with eyes and ears of a mother

Tree Life

When is a tree no longer a tree?
When it is severed from it's roots?
Skinned of its bark, its limbs hacked off?
When it falls over, a victim of age and rot?
Overwhelmed by an insect infestation?
Dries up, desiccated from lack of moisture?
It's roots flooded as rot sets in ?
Bulldozed out of existence?
Ripped apart by a chainsaw?
Suffocated in volcanic ash?
When it is burned alive in a forest fire?
When it is turned into lumber, plywood,
shingles, poles, paper?

Trees altered, transformed into man-made
objects often not acknowledged, appreciated.
Their organic heritage unrecognized
Could it be that the life-force, essence of trees
resides in our structures and objects crafted from wood?
Unlike building materials; concrete, plastic, metal,
wood is created from a living organic material,
was alive and conceivably still is.

Unlike our own mortal bodies our soul lives on
Perhaps trees also have an everlasting spirit,
which perhaps we ought awaken to.

First Contact

Morning, autumn fourteen ninety-two
Indians awaken to the early dew
A day the Arawak will come to rue
Their lives soon to be torn askew

On the horizon three-minute specks,
just perceptible as distant flecks
Within hours the objects take shape
The Indians transfixed stand and gape

In their waters anchor a windjammer
On her deck warriors suited in armour
A great vessel with sails like clouds
Spitting fire balls thundering loud

From the ships they disembark
Leaving the conquerors footmark
Who are these white skinned strangers?
A harbinger of unseen dangers?

To the Arawak sailing ships could fly
Boats and men-gods descend from the sky
Their baffling conduct and strange dress
cause the Indians unease and distress

Swords and muskets in the sunshine gleam
For the indigenous a bizarre waking dream
Ignorant of the nature of this incursion,
inevitable humiliation and submission

There will come a day we know not when
When life as we know it will come to an end
In deep space earth bound specks
just perceptible as distant specs

Within days interstellar ships take shape
As aliens disembark, we the Indians stand and gape

*"The Bible makes it clear that Adam's sin affected the whole
universe. This means that any aliens would also be affected by
Adam's sin, but because they are not Adam's descendants,
they can't have salvation."*
Ken Ham

*"Perhaps we've never been visited by aliens because they have
looked upon Earth and decided there's no sign of intelligent life."*
Neil deGrasse Tyson

Voyage

Oh, to go on a mysterious voyage
Lift the anchor, leave the moorage
Hoist the main sail, clear the deck
Sail til ship but a distant speck

Partnered with able-bodied first mate
Share the seafarer's uncertain fate
An heroic quest, the maiden voyage
calls for seafaring skill and courage
Set your compass where you're bound
lest you run your ship aground

Play the skipper, adopt the look
Sail the unknown like Captain Cook
Wind and ship roving co-conspirators
sings Rhymes of the Ancient Mariner

Glide on green and silver seascapes
Gaze on yonder foreign landscapes
Sail to remote and distant lands
Grasp greetings with foreign hands

Time and space hauntingly vast
Cross timeline to the fleeting past
Seek lost forgotten history
imbued with buried truth and mystery

Explore the contours of the mind,
there are hidden gems to find
Seek your soul's inner passage
Overboard with the old baggage
Traverse the cosmos with imagination
Pilot the ship, your dreamy creation

Vorona 1 *

Crow, a mysterious bird of duality
A clandestine life your unfortunate reality
On your nature we are divided
Held in esteem, yet scoffed and derided

Are you the bearer of good or bad tiding?
Hopes and fears on your wings are riding
Is it true you're the harbinger of death
or from the other side bring a sacred breath?

Cursed to be a marauding scavenger
You feast on carrion and cadaver
Battlefields, graveyards scoured relentlessly
Ripping, devouring road kill savagely

Unlike other birds who fly in a flock
crows are known by titles that mock
When a group is called a murder, mob or hoard
disdain for the bird is underscored

Native tribes come to your defence
Hold you in sacred reverence
A messenger from the other side
Your voice they heed and abide

Using your intelligence and character
assume the persona of 'playful trickster'
Remembering faces, using tools
you sometimes make us look like fools

Imbued with mystical spiritual meaning
between the living and dead intervening
When you enter our time and space
Change in our lives will oft take place

Will you take wing to the other side
bear witness to love ones who died?
Say I grieve and miss them so
Their loving memory in my heart aglow

Vorona – Crow in Ukrainian

Vorona 2

Every would-be writer needs a muse
Searching for one who won't refuse
Vorona, my prose is somewhat rocky
Couldn't you help this keyboard jockey?

Take me under your black wing
Please make my verses sing
Use your beak to peck a story
A tale of love, strife and glory

Guide me with your rasping caw
Put my readership in awe
We are birds of a feather
should we not work together?

Please Vorona help me out
to pen a verse to crow about

Quantum Physics

Other worldly counter intuitive findings,
the universe of Quantum Physics
Change a particle by simply observing
Be in two places at the same time
Pop in and out of existence

Imagine particles scaled up life size
to familiar Newton's rules and laws
Would it play human relations havoc?
Enhance human condition with magic?

Be in two places at the same time
Make the mundane unimaginable
Intimate conversation in your parlour
while I'm downtown, working overtime

Pop in and out of existence
Eliminate strife and discordance
Pissed off with me? I disappear
Call me back, instantly at your side

Change a particle by observing it
Custom design a bespoke partner
You observe me, transform into your heart's desire
I gaze at you, morph in what you dream me to be

"Quantum Mechanics is amazing; it is novel, profound,
mind-stretching & a very different view of reality
from what we're used to."
- Sean Carroll

Mind Meld

You said you are of two minds
Lucky you, I barely have one
Mixed signals, conflicting lines
My peace of mind slowly undone

I want inside your head, read your mind
But which one; two to choose from?
One finds me thoughtful and kind
The other, uncouth selfish numb

Fingertips to temples, a Vulcan mind meld
Crawl into your guarded psychic space
Portal to thoughts, silent secrets held
I find I hardly register, just a trace

I am not your special friend, just another
At best a minor figure, a bit player
A diminished figure just some duffer
Wish I hadn't read your mind, ego slayer

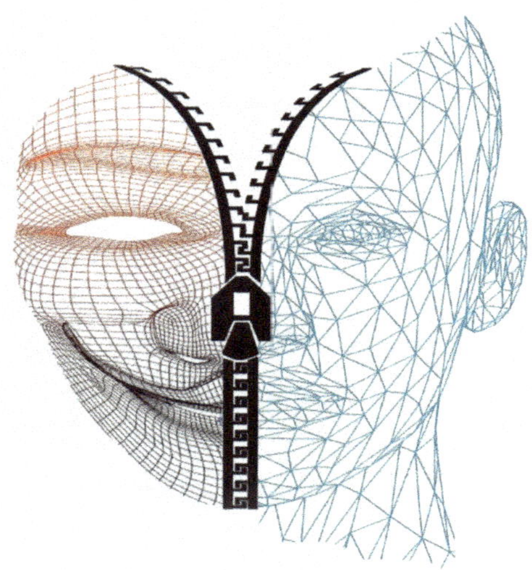

Wonderment

Oh, for a life of wonderment and mystery
Plum the depths of hidden history
Tell us stories, spin myths and tales
Shoot the breeze, make our minds sail

Silence materialists and reductionists,
the soul destroying deconstructionists
From data, facts, stats I seek to be free
Sing love lyrics that are Greek to me

See the mundane with a sense of awe
Induce boundaries of reality to thaw
Marvel at that which is delicate, feminine
Dance, sashay light footed and elegant

Reflections

"The people we are in relationships with are always a mirror, reflecting our own beliefs, and simultaneously we are mirrors, reflecting their beliefs."
- Shakti Gawain

"You realize yourself when you start reflecting - because I don't live in the past, although your past is so much a part of what you are - that you can't ignore it."
- Lauren Bacall

R.I.P Tango

She's trapped, entombed in a cardboard box
in our former backyard in a wall of grey rocks
In a place that is lonely and nondescript
her ashes repose in a stone covered crypt

Thought to bring her home to the prairie
but 'left sleeping dog lie' in her sanctuary
Now we live an ocean and mountains away
Tango on the other side will forever stay

In our memory she will always reside
Nuzzling us and ambling by our side

"Dogs come into our lives to teach us about love, they depart to teach us about loss. A new dog never replaces an old dog, it merely expands the heart."

— *Erica Jong*

Mon Amie

You ask, "I'm delicate don't you know?"
Never thought about it, guess I'm slow
"Guessing you are not as delicate as I."
Although sensitive, forgot how to cry

My incomparable friend of many decade
I, clandestine admirer master of charade
My love slowly congealing in your absence
My hopeful heart fracturing in your presence

You astutely avoid the dark, nasty, unpleasant
Dream of serenity, happiness omnipresent
Yes, Ma belle you are delicate not flimsy fragile
Wisely carry gentle feelings, brittle secrets in a satchel

You have a certain élan, warmth and generosity
Your ethereal soul aglow with luminosity
Your nickname; 'a tiny or scarcely detectable amount'
Meanness, anger, cruelty. a void none to account

Although you resist you are enhanced with age
Mature attractiveness of the feminine sage
Let's hope time has made us softer, wiser
With our affection let's not play the miser

Don't the hours grow shorter as the days go by
You never get to stop and open your eyes
One day you're waiting for the sky to fall
The next you're dazzled by the beauty of it all
Bruce Cockburn, 'Lovers in a Dangerous Time'

Dream Girl

Have you ever loved an illusion you created?
One that over time left you frustrated
You created a love object a retreating mirage
From afar a flower, in close a fading corsage

It's all on you, she isn't right yet you persisted
In quieter moments you wonder is this twisted?
She's a looker feeds the ego, a beauty, entrancing
Yet you wish she was more personable, interesting

She is what she is, a decent quiet young woman
In spite of her sex appeal she is a little dull, wooden
Perhaps I am the one who is making a stupid blunder
Forget about a dream girl I'm no dreamboat, I wonder?

Twilight Zone

Most nights I glide down a strange street
Experience that which beckons, entreat
A brief journey with ambiguity replete
A solitary sojourn, a ritualistic retreat
It is the state of the hypnagogic
World devoid of restrictive logic

The 'brainy critic' deserted home
The subconscious now free to roam
From my drowsy brainless dome the
fanciful and macabre take the throne

Uncovering

I want to undress you
Shred your protective clothing
Snip, cut, slice through cotton,
denim, rayon, polyester, lace,
wool, linen, flannel, satin

I want to undo your bindings
Pull down zippers, tug your snaps
remove clasps, undo rows of buttons
pull apart Velcro, break threads

Devoid of protective covering
Don't fear me, your exposed self
You need not try to hide
It's past time of resistance

I put my head on your breast
The living warmth of your skin
Your heart, it's rhythmic pulsation
I listen carefully, thoughtfully, tenderly
What does your heart have to say?

I am listening for the essence of you
Your hopes, fears, loves, disappointments
triumphs, crashes, leaps of imagination
the unspoken in your silence
I want to discover, decipher your soul,
further my love, strengthen our bond
For to know you is to love you.

Farewell Linda

Unearthed the last picture of you
Hijacked my world that night
The past we've been cast out of
Soft memories by dimming light

Eighteen, we would live forever
Shared fondness not to dim ever
Fork in the road, lead our own lives
Fifty years pass, stored life archives

Paths cross, serendipity, final chapter
Reminiscences shared with laughter
Months pass, urgent call from Calgary
Speak of suffering, your Calvary

Frail, enduring the last storm cloud
Fearful of the everlasting shroud
Frightened you passed away unbowed
As Donne wrote, 'death be not proud'

First Several Lines adapted from
the Pretenders, Chain Gang

Not So Close

Don't stand, don't stand so.
Don't stand so close to me
With feigned innocence
your 'onslaught' begins
The rational man overwhelmed,
a mesmerizing feminist
Your air scented flavour floods my senses
The voice in my mind silenced, stilled,
yet engrossed absorbed by you, only you

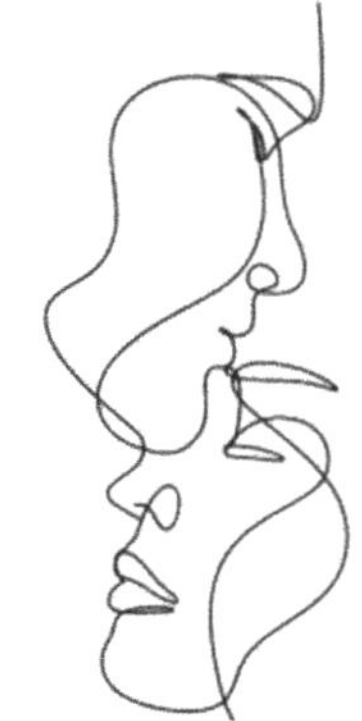

For this fleeting moment you are the drive,
the raison d'être of my being
You move ever so slightly into my space,
Our breath intermingles, absorbing
each other into our bloodstream
I reach for your hand, transfer of emotion,
finger laced feelings

We kiss, converse without words,
delight in your body heat,
the woman under the skin,
your fragile femininity,
the minuscule transfer of body fluids
For the spell of the kiss we inhabit
each other's being, charged magic

Here beneath my skin, craving,
constant craving has always been

First two lines from The Police,
 Don't Stand So Close to me
Two lines, last stanza, KD Lang, Constant Craving

An Older Man

With age intuition much improved
Details subtlety now perceived
My heart, vulnerable often moved
Wonderment, compassion readily received

What I was blind to, indifferent, suppressing
through a clearer lens I contemplate, integrate
Charitable view of humanity now developing
Cynicism, judging, my mission to abate

I can see your smile, sense your decency
The way you move, your tone, words, views
I would like to converse with you affably
Let's talk, this is no come–on sneaky ruse

I am older now, surely softer and wiser
Seek your trust, perhaps a little cheekily
Join hands share being designated driver
Commune with you happily, respectfully

Self Awareness

Unkind words I don't want to hear
Suffering I don't want to see
Poor places I don't want to go
Bitterness I don't want to taste
Wounds I don't want to touch

Lies, untruths I don't want to hear
Ignorance I don't want to endure
Hatred I don't want to encourage
Resentment I don't want to harbour
Anger I don't want to explode

Affection I want to express
Love I want to earn
Acceptance I want to realize
Fear I want to overcome
Compassion I want to learn

Patience I want to develop
Memory I want to restore
Curiosity I want to encourage
Imagination I want to flourish
Wonderment I want to experience

Young Love Angst

I once knew a woman, liked to watch her walk
Enjoyed gazing in her eyes, listen to her talk
She was my Aphrodite, but once in a life time
Decades hidden, evermore etched in my mind

Enchanted by her 'tall drink of water' beauty
Delighted in her comely, warm personality,
luscious mouth, body heat, perfumery scent
At nineteen, dreamed she was for me meant

It was not to be, much to learn love and life
When we broke our bond, regrets and strife
She took flight a fleeting shadow long gone
I lived the lyrics western heart break song